Title: "20000

As soon as she stepped into the old, abandoned building, Sarah felt an unsettling feeling in her gut. She had been hired by a local historian to explore the premises and document any significant findings. As she made her way up the stairs, she counted each step, trying to keep her mind occupied. But at the 20,000th step, something strange happened. The stairs disappeared beneath her feet, and she fell into darkness.

Sarah awoke in a dimly lit room, surrounded by musty, damp walls. She tried to get up, but found that she was bound to a rusty metal chair. A voice echoed through the darkness, promising her freedom if she could answer a riddle. The voice spoke in rhyme, and Sarah's mind raced to find the answer. But as she spoke her guess aloud, the room began to shift and change, revealing a terrifying creature.

Sarah managed to escape from the creature, but found herself trapped in a maze of endless corridors. Each turn she took seemed to lead her deeper into the maze, and further away from any hope of escape. The walls began to close in, and Sarah could hear the sound of something breathing behind her. She tried to run, but her legs felt like lead.

Finally, Sarah stumbled into a room with a large, ornate mirror. As she approached it, she saw her reflection begin to warp and distort. She tried to turn away, but her body was frozen in place. The mirror showed her visions of her deepest fears and regrets, until she could no longer bear it.

Sarah was finally able to break free from the mirror's hold, and found herself back in the stairwell. She raced down the steps, her heart pounding in her chest. As she reached the bottom, she turned to look back up at the staircase. To her horror, she saw the outline of a figure standing at the 20,000th step.

Epilogue

Years later, Sarah refused to speak about her experience in the abandoned building. The historian who had hired her was never seen again, and the building was eventually torn down. But Sarah could never forget the feeling of those 20,000 steps beneath her feet, and the horrors that lay hidden within.

Years passed since Sarah's harrowing experience in the abandoned building, but the memory continued to haunt her. She tried to forget, but the nightmares persisted, always drawing her back to that moment when the stairs disappeared beneath her feet.

Despite her best efforts, Sarah became obsessed with the building, researching its history and scouring the internet for any mention of similar occurrences. She discovered that the building had a dark past, filled with tales of murder and madness.

As she delved deeper into the building's history, Sarah began to notice strange occurrences around her. Objects moved on their own, and she would catch glimpses of shadowy figures out of the corner of her eye. She couldn't shake the feeling that she was being watched.

One night, as Sarah was going through old photographs of the building, she heard a knock at her door. When she answered it, she found a strange package waiting for her. It was a box filled with old documents and photographs, all related to the building.

As Sarah sifted through the contents, she found a letter addressed to her. It was from the historian who had hired her years ago, apologizing for leading her into danger and warning her to stay away from the building. But it was too late. Sarah was already in too deep.

The next day, Sarah drove to the site of the old building. All that remained was a pile of rubble and debris. But Sarah could sense something lurking beneath the surface, something that refused to be forgotten.

She began to dig, uncovering layer after layer of rubble and decay. And then, just as she was about to give up, she found it. A staircase leading down into the earth, with exactly 20,000 steps.

Without hesitation, Sarah descended the staircase, her heart racing with fear and anticipation. What horrors awaited her at the bottom? She didn't know, but she couldn't turn back now.

As she reached the 20,000th step, the staircase disappeared beneath her feet once again. But this time, Sarah was ready. She had faced her fears and come out the other side. Whatever lay ahead, she knew she could handle it. And so, she continued on, into the unknown.

As Sarah descended into the darkness, she felt a sense of familiarity. The maze of corridors, the shifting walls, and the mirror - all of it felt like a twisted echo of her previous experience. But this time, she was different. She was stronger, wiser, and more determined than ever before.

She navigated the maze with ease, no longer feeling the fear that had once gripped her. When she reached the mirror, she stared at her reflection with a newfound sense of confidence. She saw her past, her regrets, and her fears, but she also saw her strength, her resilience, and her hope.

As she moved through the maze, Sarah began to realize that the horrors she had once faced were not external, but internal. The building had brought out her deepest fears and insecurities, but now she had overcome them.

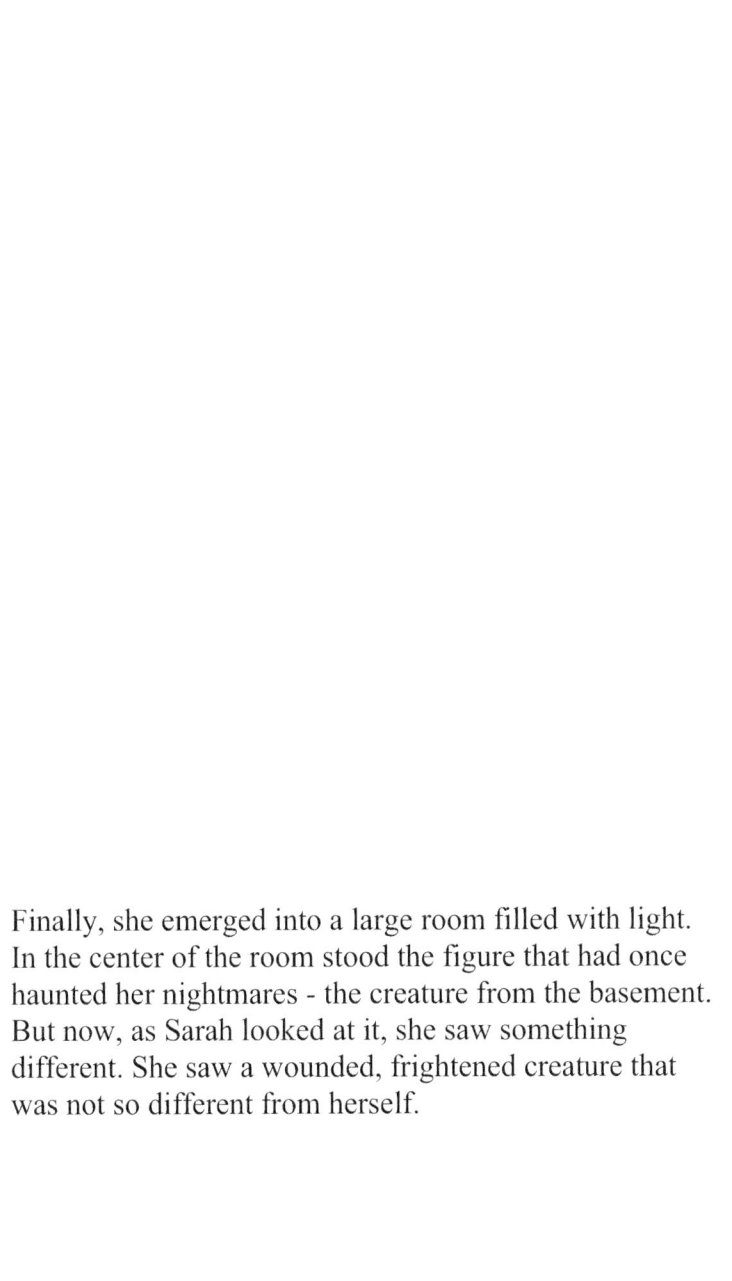

Finally, she emerged into a large room filled with light. In the center of the room stood the figure that had once haunted her nightmares - the creature from the basement. But now, as Sarah looked at it, she saw something different. She saw a wounded, frightened creature that was not so different from herself.

With compassion in her heart, Sarah approached the creature. It didn't attack her, but instead cowered away, as if expecting her to harm it. Sarah reached out her hand and touched its face, feeling its rough, scaly skin.

In that moment, something shifted. The creature transformed, its skin becoming soft and warm. It was no longer a monster, but a being of light and love. And Sarah knew, without a doubt, that she had found what she had been searching for all along - redemption.

As Sarah ascended the stairs, leaving the building behind her, she felt a sense of peace. She had faced her fears, and in doing so, had found the strength to forgive herself and others. The building was gone, but the lessons she had learned would stay with her always.

After her experience in the abandoned building, Sarah's life took on a new meaning. She no longer felt haunted by her past, but instead, she felt empowered to face her future with confidence and courage.

She returned to her job as a historian, but with a newfound appreciation for the importance of preserving history and learning from the mistakes of the past. She threw herself into her work, uncovering forgotten stories and shining a light on the hidden histories of marginalized communities.

In her personal life, Sarah found herself opening up to new experiences and relationships. She made new friends, took up new hobbies, and even started dating again. But she never forgot the lessons she had learned in the abandoned building. She remained vigilant, always on the lookout for the signs of danger, and always ready to face her fears head-on.

One day, Sarah received an unexpected package in the mail. It was a book, bound in leather and embossed with a strange symbol. There was no return address, and Sarah had no idea who had sent it to her.

She opened the book, and her heart raced as she recognized the handwriting inside. It was the historian who had hired her to explore the abandoned building all those years ago. The historian had passed away recently, and the book was his final gift to Sarah.

As she read through the pages, Sarah realized that the book was a record of the historian's own journey through the abandoned building. He had been drawn to it by a similar sense of curiosity and obsession, and he too had faced his own demons within its walls.

But what struck Sarah the most was the final entry in the book. It was a warning, a plea for future explorers to stay away from the building. The historian had realized that the building was not just a physical structure, but a metaphor for the dangers of obsession and the importance of letting go of the past.

Sarah closed the book, feeling a sense of gratitude for the gift of knowledge that the historian had given her. She knew that the lessons she had learned in the abandoned building would stay with her always, guiding her through the twists and turns of life's journey. And she knew that she would never forget the importance of facing her fears, learning from her mistakes, and letting go of the past.

Sarah placed the book on her bookshelf, feeling a sense of closure. She realized that the abandoned building had been a turning point in her life, and she was grateful for the experience. She had faced her fears and emerged stronger on the other side.

As the years went by, Sarah continued her work as a historian, uncovering forgotten stories and preserving history for future generations. She also became a mentor to young historians, passing on the lessons she had learned in her own journey.

One day, Sarah received a phone call from a colleague. He had heard about an abandoned building on the outskirts of town, and he wanted Sarah to join him in exploring it. Sarah felt a twinge of curiosity, but also a sense of caution. She knew the dangers of obsession, and she didn't want to fall into the same trap again.

But as she thought about it more, she realized that the experience had given her the strength to face whatever challenges lay ahead. She agreed to join her colleague, but with a newfound sense of perspective and caution.

As they approached the building, Sarah felt a sense of Deja vu. The same sense of unease and curiosity that had drawn her to the abandoned building so many years ago was now tugging at her once again. But this time, she was prepared.

Together with her colleague, Sarah explored the abandoned building, but with a sense of caution and respect. She saw the same shifting walls and maze-like corridors, but this time, she knew that they were just physical structures, not metaphors for her own fears and insecurities.

As they made their way through the building, Sarah realized that she had come full circle. She had faced her fears and emerged stronger on the other side, and now, she was able to explore the abandoned building without being consumed by obsession.

As they emerged from the building, Sarah felt a sense of peace. She knew that the lessons she had learned would stay with her always, guiding her through whatever challenges lay ahead. And she knew that, no matter what, she would always be able to face her fears and emerge stronger on the other side.

As Sarah and her colleague walked away from the abandoned building, they were both silent. It was as if they were processing the experience they had just shared. Sarah couldn't help but reflect on how far she had come since her first exploration of the building. She had faced her fears, learned from her mistakes, and had grown in so many ways.

As they walked down the street, Sarah's colleague turned to her and said, "You know, Sarah, you're one of the strongest people I know. I admire your courage and resilience." Sarah felt a sense of gratitude and pride welling up inside of her. She knew that she had worked hard to get to where she was, and it felt good to be recognized for it.

From that day on, Sarah continued to grow and thrive. She continued her work as a historian, mentoring others and uncovering forgotten stories. She also took on new challenges, like traveling to new countries and trying new things.

But most importantly, Sarah never forgot the lessons she had learned in the abandoned building. She knew that life was full of challenges and obstacles, but she also knew that she was strong enough to face them. She had the courage, resilience, and determination to overcome whatever came her way.

Years later, Sarah found herself back in the abandoned building once again. This time, she was leading a group of young historians on a tour of the building. She saw the same shifting walls and maze-like corridors, but this time, she was calm and confident. She was able to guide the young historians through the building with ease, sharing her knowledge and experience with them.

As they emerged from the building, Sarah felt a sense of pride and satisfaction. She knew that she had come full circle, and that she had truly grown in so many ways. She had faced her fears, learned from her mistakes, and had become the person she always knew she could be.

As Sarah led the group of young historians away from the abandoned building, she couldn't help but smile. She had come a long way since her first exploration of the building. She had faced her fears, learned from her mistakes, and had grown in so many ways.

But more than that, Sarah realized that the journey never truly ends. There would always be new challenges to face, new obstacles to overcome, and new lessons to learn. But now, she knew that she had the strength and resilience to face whatever lay ahead.

And as she looked at the group of young historians following behind her, she felt a sense of purpose. She knew that she had a responsibility to pass on the lessons she had learned, to guide and mentor the next generation of historians.

Sarah continued to thrive in her work, uncovering forgotten stories and preserving history for future generations. She also continued to face new challenges and overcome new obstacles, always with a sense of purpose and determination.

And years later, when Sarah was an old woman, she would look back on her life with pride and gratitude. She would remember the abandoned building and the lessons it had taught her, and she would know that she had truly lived a life of courage and resilience.

As Sarah grew older, she continued to pass on her knowledge and experience to the next generation of historians. She wrote books, gave lectures, and mentored young people, always encouraging them to face their fears and pursue their passions.

And even as she approached the end of her life, Sarah never lost her sense of purpose. She knew that the lessons she had learned in the abandoned building would stay with her forever, guiding her through the final stages of her journey.

As Sarah lay on her deathbed, surrounded by loved ones, she felt a sense of peace. She knew that she had lived a full and meaningful life, and that she had made a difference in the world.

And as she closed her eyes for the final time, Sarah saw in her mind's eye the shifting walls and maze-like corridors of the abandoned building. But this time, she saw them not as symbols of fear and uncertainty, but as a reminder of all that she had overcome.

And with a smile on her face, Sarah slipped away, knowing that she had faced her fears and emerged stronger on the other side. And that, she knew, was the greatest gift of all.

The End